ANTHONY REYNOSO:
BORN TO
Rope

BY MARTHA COOPER
& GINGER GORDON

CLARION BOOKS / NEW YORK

CLARION BOOKS
a Houghton Mifflin Company imprint
215 Park Avenue South, New York, NY 10003
Text copyright © 1996 by Ginger Gordon
Photographs copyright © 1996 by Martha Cooper

Type is 14-point Sabon.
Book design by Sylvia Frezzolini Severance

For information about this and other Houghton Mifflin trade
and reference books and multimedia products, visit The
Bookstore at Houghton Mifflin on the World Wide Web at
(http://www.hmco.com/trade/).

Printed in Hong Kong

Library of Congress Cataloging-in-Publication Data

Cooper, Martha.
    Anthony Reynoso : born to rope / [by Martha Cooper
and Ginger Gordon.]
        p.   cm.
    ISBN 0-395-71690-X
    1. Reynoso, Anthony—Juvenile literature. 2. Cowboys—
United States—Biography—Juvenile literature. 3. Trick Roping—
United States—Juvenile literature. 4. Rodeos—United States—
Juvenile literature.   I. Gordon, Ginger.   II. Title.
GV1833.6.R49C66   1996
791.8'4'092—dc20   95-24434
[B]   CIP
                                                               AC
CLR   10 9 8 7 6 5 4 3 2 1

ACKNOWLEDGMENTS: This book is a result of the cooperation,
hospitality, and participation of many wonderful people including
Anthony's grandparents, Antonio and Roberta Reynoso; his par-
ents, Elizabeth and Anthony; his aunts and uncles, Janelle,
Anjelica, Yvette, Roberta, Joann, Robert, Xavier, Belinda, Noe,
and Annette; and his cousins, Champ, Xavier Jr., Feanna, Eliana,
Tatiana, Jonathan, Erica, and Darien. We thank Michelle Corabi,
Anthony's fourth grade teacher at his public school Kyrene del
Norte, and his classmates Andy and Ramon Guzman, and
Natalie Curtis who welcomed us into their classroom. Thanks as
well to the Mariachi Colonial de Guadalupe Esparza and the
Ballet Folklorico Infantil. We appreciate the generosity of Walt
Guthrie and John Ahearn in being our Phoenix connection.

This book is dedicated
to *charros* past, present,
and future.

ℳy name is Anthony Reynoso. I'm named after my father, who is holding the white horse, and my grandfather, who is holding the dappled horse. We all rope and ride Mexican Rodeo style on my grandfather's ranch outside of Phoenix, Arizona.

As soon as I could stand, my dad gave me a rope. I had my own little hat and everything else I needed to dress as a *charro*. That's what a Mexican cowboy is called.

It's a good thing I started when I was little, because it takes years to learn to rope.

I live with my mom and dad in the little Mexican-American and
Yaqui Indian town of Guadalupe. All my grandparents live close by.
This will help a lot when the new baby comes. My mom is pregnant.

I've got a secret
about Guadalupe.
I know where there
are petroglyphs in
the rocks right near
my house. My
favorite looks like
a man with a shield.
People carved these
petroglyphs hundreds
of years ago. Why did
they do it? I wonder
what the carvings
mean.

Every Sunday morning the old Mexican Mission church is packed.

At Easter, lots of people come to watch the Yaqui Indian ceremonies in the center of town. No one's allowed to take photographs, but an artist painted this wall showing the Yaqui dancers.

Some Sundays, we go to Casa Reynoso, my grandparents' restaurant. If it's very busy, my cousins and I pitch in. When there's time, my grandmother lets me help in the kitchen. Casa Reynoso has the best Mexican food in town.

On holidays, we go to my grandfather's ranch. Once a year, we all get dressed up for a family photo.

I've got lots of cousins. Whenever there's a birthday we have a piñata. We smash it with a stick until all the candy falls out.

Then we
scramble to
grab as much
as we can
hold.

Best of all, at the ranch we get to practice roping on horseback.
My dad's always trying something new . . .

and so am I!
In Mexico, the Rodeo is the national sport. The most famous charros there are like sports stars here.

On weekdays, Dad runs his landscape business, Mom works in a public school, and I go to school. I wait for the bus with other kids at the corner of my block.

I always come to school with my homework done. When I'm in class, I forget about roping and riding. I don't think anyone in school knows about it except my best friends.

It's different when I get home. I practice hard with Dad. He's a good teacher and shows me everything his father taught him. We spend a lot of time practicing for shows at schools, malls, and rodeos. We are experts at passing the rope. Our next big exhibition is in Sedona, about two hours away by car.

After rope practice we shoot a few baskets. Dad's pretty good at that too!

On Friday after school, Dad and I prepare our ropes for the show in Sedona. They've got to be just right.

Everything's ready for tomorrow, so I can take a break and go through my basketball cards. I decide which ones I want to buy, sell, and trade. Collecting basketball cards is one of my favorite hobbies.

It's Saturday! Time for the show in Sedona. I get a little nervous watching the other performers. I sure wouldn't want to get messed up in my own rope in front of all these people!

After the Mexican hat dance, we're next!

My dad goes first . . .

and then it's my turn. While the mariachis play, I do my stuff.

Even Dad can't spin the rope from his teeth like this!

Then Dad and I rope together, just like we practiced. It's hard to do with our wide charro hats on. When my dad passes the rope to me and I spin it well, he says he has passed the Mexican Rodeo tradition on to me. Now it's up to me to keep it going.

Mom is our best fan. She always comes with us. It makes me feel good to know she's out there watching.

Sometimes tourists want us to pose for pictures with them. It makes me feel like a celebrity.

After the show, boy, are we hungry! We pack up and eat a quick lunch. Then we go to a special place called Slide Rock.

Slide Rock is a natural water slide where kids have played for
hundreds, maybe even thousands, of years. It's cold today!
I'd rather come back in the summer when it's hot.

But Dad pulls me
in anyway. Brrr!

Time to go home.
Next time we
come to Sedona,
the baby will be
with us. I wonder
if it will be a boy
or a girl. It's hard
to wait!

I'm going to love being a big brother. Pretty soon the baby will be wearing my old boots and learning how to rope from me.